King of the Jungle

written by **Anne Giulieri**

illustrated by **Louise Gardner**

One day Baby Elephant
was playing in the water.

Little Leo ran by.
He was running very fast.

"Look at me!"
shouted Little Leo.
"I am running very fast."

Then off he ran into the jungle.

"Come back!"
shouted Baby Elephant.
"I am having fun in the water.
Come back and play with me."

"No!" said Little Leo.
"I cannot play with you.
I have to run fast.
One day I will be
King of the Jungle."

"Can I run in the jungle with you?" said Baby Elephant.

"No!" said Little Leo.
"You cannot run with me.
You are **not** fast."

Little Leo ran and ran.

He ran in and out of the jungle.

He did not stop.

"I am **very** hot!"
said Little Leo.
"I will **have** to stop."

"Little Leo,"
said Baby Elephant.
"I cannot run fast like you.
But I **can** help you!"

Baby Elephant got his long trunk.
The long trunk went
down, down, down.

Then his long trunk went
up, up, up.

Whoooosh!

Lots of water came out!

"This is lots of fun,"
said Little Leo.
"I like playing with you!"